Little Grey Rabbit's Christmas

Alison Uttley
pictures by Margaret Tempest

Butterscotch Books

Published by Advanced Marketing Services, Inc.
San Diego, CA
First published 1939
Text copyright © The Alison Uttley Literary Property Trust 1986.
Illustrations copyright © The Estate of Margaret Tempest 1986.
This arrangement © William Collins Sons & Co Ltd 1988.
All rights reserved.
Decorated capital by Mary Cooper

Alison Uttley's original story has been abridged for this book.
Printed in Belgium by Proost International Book Production
Butterscotch Books™
All rights reserved.
ISBN 0-934429-09-X
1   2   3   4   5   6   7   8   9

FOREWORD

Of course you must understand that Grey Rabbit's home had no electric light or gas. The candles were made from the pith of rushes dipped in wax from the wild bees' nests, which Squirrel had found. Water there was in plenty, but it did not come from a faucet. It flowed from a spring outside, which rose up from this ground and went to a brook. Grey Rabbit cooked on a wood fire for there was no coal in that part of the country. Tea did not come from India, but from a little herb known very well to country people, who dried it and used it in their cottage homes. Bread was baked from finely ground wheat ears, which Hare and Grey Rabbit gleaned in the cornfields.

The doormats were braided rushes, like country-made mats, and cushions were stuffed with wool gathered from the hedges where sheep had pushed through the thorns. As for the looking-glass, Grey Rabbit found the glass, which had dropped from a lady's handbag, and Mole made a frame for it. Usually the animals gazed at themselves in the still pools as so many country children have done. The country ways of Grey Rabbit were the country ways known to the author.

t had been snowing for hours. Hare stood in the garden of the little house at the end of the woods, watching the snowflakes tumbling down like white feathers from the gray sky.

"Whatever are you doing, Hare?" cried Squirrel, who stayed close to the fire. "Come in! You'll catch cold."

"I am catching cold, and eating it too," replied Hare, happily.

"Hare! How long do you think Grey Rabbit will be? Can you see her coming? What is she doing?" called Squirrel again.

"She's at the market, buying Christmas fare for all of us," replied Hare, as he caught an extra large snowflake on his red tongue.

As he spoke, a small stout animal came trudging up the lane, carrying a heavy basket and a bulging string bag. Straggling behind was a little snow-covered creature.

"There she is!" cried Hare, leaping forward. "Make the tea, Squirrel."

He ran down the path, and then stopped, disappointed. "It's only Mrs. Hedgehog!" he muttered. "And Fuzzypeg," he added, as he recognized the little fellow.

"Have you seen little Grey Rabbit?" asked Hare, leaning over the gate.

"I have indeed," said Mrs. Hedgehog, resting her burden on the snow. "She was at the market along with me. Then she went to talk to Old Joe the Carpenter."

"What did she want with Joe?" asked Hare.

"Please Sir!" cried Fuzzypeg. "I know, Sir. I know what Grey Rabbit went to the Carpenter for."

"Sh-sh!" Mrs. Hedgehog shook her head at her son. "You mustn't let the cat out of the bag." Then, picking up her basket, she continued on her way, with little Fuzzypeg protesting, "There wasn't a cat in the bag, Mother. There wasn't."

It was growing dark when Squirrel and Hare
heard the sound of merry voices and the
ringing of bells.

They ran to the door, and there was a fine
scarlet sled drawn by two young rabbits, with
little Grey Rabbit herself sitting cozily on
the top!

"Oh, Grey Rabbit, what a lovely sled!"
cried Squirrel, as she rubbed her paws over the
smooth sides.

"Grey Rabbit! Our names are on it!"
shouted Hare.

He pointed excitedly to the words,
"Squirrel, Hare and little Grey Rabbit"
written around the sides. "It's ours. It says so!"

"Yes. It is our very own," said Grey Rabbit.
"I ordered it from Joe Carpenter, and these
kind rabbits insisted on bringing me home."

After breakfast the next day, Squirrel and Grey Rabbit sat on the sled, and Hare pulled them over the field.

They came to their favorite hill. Hare mounted behind them and stretched out his long legs.

"One to be ready!

"Two to be steady!

"Three to be off!" he cried, and away they went down the steep slope.

"Whoo-oo-oo!" cried Hare. "What speed! Whoops! Whoa!"

But the sled wouldn't stop.

At last it struck a molehill, and over they all toppled, head over heels.

"Sixty miles an hour!" cried Hare, sitting up and rubbing his elbow.

Little Fuzzypeg, carrying a slice of bread and jam, came to watch the fun. He stared at the three dragging their sled up the slope.

"I want to toboggan," he said, softly, but nobody heard. "Look at me toboggan! Watch me!" cried Fuzzypeg. He made himself into a ball and rolled down the hill, faster and faster. When he got to the bottom there was no Fuzzypeg to be seen, only an enormous snowball.

"What a big snowball!" cried Squirrel, climbing off the sled.

"What a beauty!" exclaimed Grey Rabbit.

"Help! Help!" squeaked a tiny voice. "Get me out!"

"What's that?" cried Squirrel.

"Help! Help!" squeaked Fuzzypeg.

"It's a talking snowball," said Hare. "Isn't that interesting? I shall take it home and keep it in the garden."

He dragged the large ball onto the sled and pulled the load uphill. When he reached the top, Hare rolled the ball to the ground and gave it a kick.

"Ouch!" he cried, limping. "There's a thorn inside."

"Help! Help!" shrieked the tiny faraway voice. "Let me out!"

"That's like Fuzzypeg's voice," said Grey Rabbit, and she bent over and loosened the caked snow.

Out came the little hedgehog, eating his bread and jam.

"However did you get inside a snowball?" asked Hare.

"I didn't get inside. It got around me," replied Fuzzypeg. "Can I go on your sled now?"

Hare took the little hedgehog for a ride, but when Fuzzypeg flung his arms around Hare's waist, he sprang away shrieking.

"That's enough," Hare said.

Fuzzypeg ran home and returned with a tea tray. After him came a crowd of rabbits, each carrying a tray, and they all rode helter-skelter down the slope, shouting and laughing as they tried to race each other.

Squirrel, Hare and little Grey Rabbit took
their sled to Moldy Warp's house. Squirrel
ran up the holly trees and gathered sprigs of
the blazing red berries. Mole came out and
showed them the mistletoe growing on an oak
tree. And then he helped them to tie their
branches on the sled.

They said good-bye and hurried home.

Hare shut the sled in the woodshed and
carried the holly and mistletoe indoors. Grey
Rabbit stood at the table making mince pies,
and Hare and Squirrel decorated the room.
They popped sprigs on the clock, over the
corner cupboard, around the warming pan,
and among the mugs on the sideboard.

Little Grey Rabbit looked up from her patty-pans and waved her rolling pin to direct operations.

Up the lane came a little group, carrying rolls of music and pipes of straw. They talked softly as they walked up to the closed door of Grey Rabbit's house. They arranged themselves in a circle, coughed and cleared their throats, and held up their music to the moonlight.

"Now then, altogether!" cried an important-looking rabbit, playing a note on his straw pipe. "One, two, three!" and with their noses in the air they began to sing in small squeaky voices:

"Holly red and mistletoe white,
The stars are shining with golden light,
Burning like candles this Holy Night.
Holly red and mistletoe white."

"Hush! What's that noise?" cried Hare,
dropping his mistletoe.

"It's the Waits!" said Grey Rabbit, and she
held up her wooden spoon.

They flung open the door and saw the little
group of rabbits and hedgehogs, peering at
their sheets of music.

"Come in! Come in!" cried Grey Rabbit.
"Come in and sing by the fireside. You look
frozen with the cold."

"We're all right," said a big rabbit, "but a
warm drink would wet our whistles."

Grey Rabbit took the two-handled Christmas mug of primrose wine from the fire, and the carollers passed it around.

Then they stood by the fire and sang all the songs they knew: "The Moon Shines Bright," "I Saw Three Ships A-Sailing," and "Green Grows The Holly."

"Now we must be off," they said, after Grey Rabbit had given them hot mince pies. "We have to sing at all the rabbit houses tonight. Good night. Happy Christmas!"

Squirrel, Hare and little Grey Rabbit stood watching the Waits as they crossed the fields. As they trotted along, the animals sang "Holly Red and Mistletoe White."

"I think I shall take the sled and toboggan
down the hill by moonlight," said Hare.

He seized the cord of the sled and ran across
the fields to the hill.

Then down he swooped, flying like a bird.

Again and again he rushed down, his eyes
on the lovely moon. Suddenly he noticed a
dark shadow running alongside. It was his
own shadow, but Hare saw the long ears of a
strange monster.

"Oh dear! Oh dear! Who is that fellow
racing by my side?" he cried.

He took to his heels and hurried home,
leaving the sled lying in the field.

"Did you come without the sled?" asked
Squirrel. "Hare, you are a coward! I don't
believe there was anybody there at all."

"You ran away from your shadow. You've lost our lovely sled!"

"Better than losing my lovely life," retorted Hare. He felt rather miserable. "I suppose we had better go to bed," he muttered. "I don't suppose there will be any presents tomorrow. I don't think Santa Claus will find this house with so much snow!"

He went upstairs gloomily, but he hung up his furry stocking all the same, and so did Squirrel.

When all was quiet Grey Rabbit slipped out of bed. Under her bed were several packages. She opened them and filled the stockings with sugarplums and lollipops. Then she ran downstairs to the kitchen, where the dying fire flickered softly.

She tied together little sprays of holly and made a round ball called a Kissing Bunch. Then she hung it from a hook in the ceiling.

On Christmas morning Grey Rabbit was so sleepy she didn't wake up till Hare burst into her room.

"Grey Rabbit! Merry Christmas! He's been here! Wake up! He's been here in the night!"

"Who?" cried Grey Rabbit.

"Santa Claus!" cried Hare. "Quick! Come downstairs and see."

Grey Rabbit dressed hurriedly and entered the kitchen.

"Look at the Kissing Bunch!" said Hare. "Isn't it lovely! Let's all kiss under it."

So they gave their Christmas morning kisses under the round Christmas Bunch.

Robin the Postman flew to the door with some Christmas cards and a letter. The little bird rested and ate some breakfast while Hare examined the letter.

"It's from Mole," he said.

"Yes, I know," replied Robin. "Mole gave it to me."

"You're reading it upside down, Hare!" cried Squirrel. She took the little letter and read, "Come tonight. Love from Moldy Warp."

"It's a party!" cried Hare. "Quick, Grey Rabbit! Write and say we'll come."

Grey Rabbit sat at her desk and wrote on an ivy leaf, "Thank you dear Moldy Warp."

Then away flew Robin with the leaf in his bag.

All day they enjoyed themselves, playing
Musical Chairs, pulling tiny poppers, and
crunching lollipops.

In the evening they all trooped to the hill
to look for the sled, but it wasn't there. Snow
had covered all traces of footprints.

"Santa Claus has borrowed it," said Grey
Rabbit. "When the snow melts we shall
find it."

The first star appeared in the sky, and the
three animals wrapped themselves up in warm
clothes, and set off for Mole's house. They
carried presents for the lonely Mole, and some
of their own Christmas fare.

"What a pity you lost our sled. We could
have ridden on it tonight," said Squirrel
to Hare.

When the three got near Mole's house they
saw something glittering. A lighted tree grew
by the path.

"Oh dear! Something's on fire!" cried Hare.
"Let's put it out."

"Hush!" whispered Grey Rabbit. "It's a
magical tree."

On every branch of the tree, candles
flickered. On the ground under the branches
were bowls of nuts, round loaves of bread,
piles of cakes, and small sacks of corn. There
were jars of honey as big as thimbles, and
bottles of heather ale.

"What do you think of my tree?" asked
Moldy Warp, stepping out of the shadows.

"Is it a Fairy Tree?" asked Grey Rabbit.

"It's a Christmas Tree," replied Mole. "It's for
all the birds and beasts of the woods and fields.
Now sit quietly and watch."

Across the snowy fields padded little

creatures, all filled with curiosity to see the glowing tree.

"Help yourselves," cried Mole, waving his short arms. "It's Christmas. Eat, drink and warm yourselves."

From behind a tree Rat sidled toward Grey
Rabbit.

"Miss Grey Rabbit," said he. "I found a
scarlet sled in the field last night, and as your
family name was on it, I took the liberty of
bringing it here."

"Oh, thank you, kind Rat," cried Grey
Rabbit, clapping her paws. "The sled is found!
Come Hare! Squirrel! Moldy Warp!"

The scarlet sled was clean and bright and
on the top was a fleecy shawl. From under it
Grey Rabbit drew three objects. The first was a
walking stick made of holly wood. The second
was a little wooden spoon. The third was a
tiny bone box, and when Grey Rabbit opened
the lid there was a little thimble inside which
exactly fitted her.

"I haven't had a thimble since Wise Owl swallowed mine," she said happily.

"Good Santa Claus," cried Hare. "He knew what we wanted."

"Only one person could make such delicate carvings," said Grey Rabbit.

"And that is Rat," said Squirrel.

"Three cheers for Rat!" cried Fuzzypeg, and they all cheered, "Hip! Hip! Hooray!"

Squirrel and Grey Rabbit climbed on the sled, and Hare pulled them over the snow.

"Good night. A happy Christmas!" they called.

"The same to you," answered Moldy Warp. The Hedgehog family waved and shouted, "Merry Christmas!"

"Heigh-ho! I'm sleepy," murmured Squirrel,
"but it has been lovely. Thank you everyone
for a happy day."

She curled down under the fleecy shawl by
Grey Rabbit's side, clutching her wooden
spoon. Grey Rabbit sat wide awake, her
thimble was on her finger, her eyes shone with
happiness.

Hare ran swiftly over the frozen snow,
drawing the scarlet sled toward the little house
at the end of the woods.

Mistletoe white and holly red,
The day is over, we're off to bed,
Tired body and sleepy head,
Mistletoe white and holly red.